WITHDRAWN

The Adventures of Sam X

RETURNING THE HUNTER'S STONE

by Hubert Ben Kemoun

illustrated by Thomas Ehretsmann

translated by Genevieve Chamberland

MORRIS AREA LIBRARY

STONE ARCH BOOKS
www.stonearchbooks.com

First published in the United States in 2009
by Stone Arch Books,
151 Good Counsel Drive, P.O. Box 669
Mankato, Minnesota 56002
www.stonearchbooks.com

Copyright © 2006 Éditions Nathan, Paris, France
Original editon: *Maudit jardin!*

All rights reserved. No part of this publication may be reproduced
in whole or in part, or stored in a retrieval system, or transmitted
in any form or by any means, electronic, mechanical, photocopying,
recording, or otherwise, without written permission of the publisher.

Library of Congress Cataloging-in-Publication Data
Ben Kemoun, Hubert, 1958–
    [Maudit jardin. English]
    Returning the Hunter's Stone / by Hubert Ben Kemoun; illustrated by
Thomas Ehretsmann.
    p. cm. — (Pathway Books Editions. The Adventures of Sam X)
    Originally published: Maudit jardin. France: Nathan, 2008.
    ISBN 978-1-4342-1221-4 (library binding)
    [1. Rocks—Fiction. 2. Supernatural—Fiction.] I. Ehretsmann, Thomas,
ill. II. Title.
PZ7.B4248Re 2009
[Fic]—dc22   2008031580

Summary: When Sam's uncle comes back from the Amazon and gives him
a boring blue stone, Sam is disappointed. But when he climbs over a wall
into a deserted back yard to retrieve a missing ball, things get wild! Sam
soon finds himself being chased through an Amazonian jungle — and the
strange blue stone may be the one thing that can save him!

Creative Director: Heather Kindseth
Graphic Designer: Emily Harris

1 2 3 4 5 6 14 13 12 11 10 09

Printed in the United States of America

TABLE OF CONTENTS

3 9957 00146 2981

Chapter 1

UNCLE JULIUS RETURNS

My uncle Julius was an explorer. For years, he had been traveling the world from one end to the other. He searched all over the planet for new species of flowers and trees.

He hardly ever came to visit, but whenever he did, it was magical.

I loved it when Uncle Julius was visiting. Having him in our house was better than a brand new video game or watching all of my favorite TV shows in one night. I loved hearing about his crazy expeditions in the desert or the jungle.

My mom said that the stuff Uncle Julius brought back was junk. She said it belonged in a trash can.

Sometimes he'd bring back seeds or pieces of roots in his suitcase. Mom would roll her eyes and say it looked like garbage.

Uncle Julius told us that famous scientists were fighting for the things that he found. He said they all wanted to pay a lot of money for his discoveries.

The best thing about Uncle Julius's visits were the stories he told. He always told me some really crazy stories. I loved hearing them.

Uncle Julius's stories took place all over the world. He was always getting into trouble, and then finding his way out of it. He had only his smarts as a weapon.

That night, his first night in our apartment after being away for months, he was in the middle of a great story.

"I walked into a thick forest for six days and six nights," he said. "I had lost my maps, and I was alone. I was following a creek. I knew it had to end up somewhere."

"How did you know?" I asked.

Uncle Julius tapped his nose. "I just knew," he said. "Then, on the seventh day of my journey, I found a desert village and a trail."

He took a deep breath. Then he went on, "Finally, a real trail! Everyone knows all trails lead to cities — the trail would bring me closer to my nephew!"

Uncle Julius smiled. Then he messed up my hair with his big hand.

I wanted the story to keep going. I wished that the clock in the living room would stop so it would never be time for bed.

Uncle Julius's stories are even better than the very best dreams. I wanted to hear more stories about the time he was in the rain forest and he almost died a thousand times.

But then my mom said the same, awful, boring thing she says every night. She looked at her watch and said, "You have school tomorrow, Samuel. It's time for bed now."

I tried to beg. "Just let me stay up for five more minutes," I said. "Just to hear one more story."

My mom shook her head. "Uncle Julius is here for eight more days," she said. "You'll have plenty of time to hear lots of his stories."

Uncle Julius slapped his forehead. "I forgot the best part, Sam!" he said. "I brought you a souvenir." He reached for one of his big bags, waiting in the corner of the living room.

He bent over and dug through the bag. When he stood up, he was holding a rough leather cord. A big, bright blue stone was on the cord.

Uncle Julius handed it to me. "The people who live in the Amazon call this stone the Kaan," he said. "When one of them goes hunting, he covers it with mud and wears it around his neck. That way, he becomes one with the Earth, the Sky, the Water — all of nature."

"Cool," I said quietly.

Uncle Julius went on, "The legend says that because of those mysterious stones, the natives are masters of the Great Forest and nothing can happen to them. This is the first time a Kaan has been brought out of the Amazon! And it's all yours!"

I looked down at the leather cord and bright blue bead. I felt disappointed.

"Thanks, Uncle Julius," I said. Then I went to my room.

I felt confused and upset as I got ready for bed.

My uncle had been on the other side of the world. Couldn't he have brought me a bow and arrow, or a slingshot, or some poison or something? Why did he bring me a necklace?

I looked at the blue stone again before I got into bed. It seemed like a present for a girl.

It wasn't a good present for someone like me. It wasn't a gift for someone who was an adventurer and explorer. Someone brave.

I shoved the Kaan in the pocket of a pair of pants on my bedroom floor. I didn't know then how wrong I was about the blue stone.

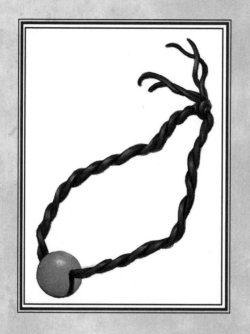

Chapter 2

TWO APPLE TREES

"Do you see it?" Lionel asked.

"No," I said, "but it can't be far. This yard is so little! But there's a lot of tall grass and bushes. Your ball must be in there. I'll go find it."

I was standing on Lionel's shoulders and gripping the top of a stone wall.

The wall stood around an old house next to the river. Lionel's ball had flown over the wall, and I was trying to figure out where it had landed. No one lived in the house, so I wasn't worried about getting in trouble.

"Hurry up," Lionel said. "You're not that heavy, but I'm going to drop you soon."

"I'll go over there and get your ball back," I told him. "After all, I'm the one who kicked it too hard and too high. It's my fault, so I'll go and get it."

I pulled myself to the top of the wall. My pants ripped on a jagged stone. I sat down on the top of the wall.

"How are you going to climb back up the wall from the other side?" Lionel asked. He rubbed his shoulders where I'd been standing.

I looked down at the other side. "The wall is in pretty bad shape over here," I told him. "There will be spots I can grab onto. Climbing back over won't be hard. Don't worry."

I took a breath. Then I said, "Okay, I'm going to jump!"

"Be careful!" shouted Lionel. I slid off of the wall and landed in the yard.

I was used to Lionel worrying too much, but it still annoyed me. He was always worrying and telling me to be careful.

There was no reason to be careful in this yard. The yard only had two twisty, old apple trees and a bunch of blackberry bushes.

There wasn't anything to worry about. I'd find the ball quickly and climb back out of there.

I heard Lionel from the other side of the wall. "Do you see it? Did you find it?" he asked. I could tell he was losing his patience. "Come on, Sam, hurry up," he added.

"I just started looking!" I yelled back. "Give me a couple of minutes. Just calm down!"

I started walking through the yard. Some of the grass was as tall as I was. It seemed like it hadn't been mowed in years.

I looked down with each step, trying to find Lionel's ball. Maybe I would find it lying somewhere in the thick, tall grass.

I gazed around the yard. Ahead of me was part of an old, broken-down building. The river was to my left, lined with some bushes. Behind me stood the big stone wall.

"Did you find it yet?" Lionel yelled again.

I rolled my eyes. "Just hold on," I said. "I don't see it yet, but it must be around here somewhere. We saw it go over the wall and into this yard."

I had thought it would be really easy to find the missing ball. But it wasn't easy at all.

Even though the ball was black and white, it was hard to spot in the middle of this miniature jungle.

I walked straight ahead, looking carefully at the ground as I walked. I stomped down the grass, creating a path. There were prickly things everywhere, scratching my arms and legs.

Buzzing insects were all around me. I tried to pretend they weren't there.

I felt like a hunter in the Amazon. That made me remember the Kaan in my pocket.

I put my hand into my pocket to touch the blue stone my uncle had given me two days earlier. But the Kaan had disappeared.

I shrugged. I had probably dropped it earlier while Lionel and I were playing soccer.

Then I heard Lionel's voice. "Sam, are you okay?" he yelled. "Hey, Sam, what's going on over there?"

I jumped and turned around. I stared at the wall.

I wasn't startled that Lionel was calling to me. I was startled because his voice seemed so far away.

It sounded like he was miles away, but I was sure I had only walked a few feet since I jumped off the wall.

That's what I thought, anyway! I turned around and gasped. The wall was at least a hundred feet away!

I started to panic. I could feel myself start shaking. I looked around, trying to figure out what had happened.

Something else was strange. Before, I had only seen two apple trees in the yard. Now I could see that there were at least ten big tree trunks standing there, being choked by a bunch of thick bushes.

Chapter 3

GIGANTIC!

I've never been that good at knowing how far away something is. I'm also bad at telling how tall someone is or how big something is. But I knew that I hadn't taken more than ten steps since I went over the wall.

I tried to tell myself I had just walked more than I thought. Or that I'd walked faster than I thought.

I tried to believe that from the top of the wall, the yard had just looked much smaller, and that I hadn't counted some of the apple trees.

But I knew that wasn't true.

The grass I was standing in seemed to have grown much taller and thicker. The prickly thorns on the bushes also seemed sharper.

The broken-down old house was hard to see through the thick grass. It seemed like the house was farther away than I had thought, too.

Was I going crazy?

Behind me, the grass I had stomped down was showing me the way back to the wall.

I should have turned around and headed back. But at the time, it didn't seem like the right thing to do.

I didn't want to admit that the yard was starting to scare me. I didn't want to tell Lionel that I felt like I was losing my mind!

From very far away, I heard Lionel's voice again. "Sam, what are you doing?" he yelled. "Sam? Can you hear me?"

Then I remembered why I was in the yard to begin with. I had to find Lionel's ball!

I was going to get back to my search when I saw a tarantula walk by. It was just inches away from my shoes.

It was an enormous bug. It was as big as a plate. It was as hairy as a cat. It stopped to look at the end of my shoelace, which was touching the ground.

I ran away as fast as I could, screaming.

There are not supposed to be tarantulas where I live. Maybe there's one at the zoo or the natural history museum, but there are definitely not supposed to be any tarantulas loose in the wild!

I stopped to catch my breath. I was covered in sweat. I was completely lost. I felt weird, like millions of eyes were looking at me.

Then I noticed a swarm of red ants marching toward me. Each of the ants was as big as a grasshopper. I started to run again.

Running reminded me of having a nightmare. That's what I felt like — like I was trapped in the middle of a nightmare.

But I was fully awake. It was the middle of the afternoon. I wasn't sleeping. It wasn't a bad dream.

I just kept running.

The tall grass whipped against my arms and legs. The sun was shining, but I barely noticed.

Then I stopped. I turned around and looked at the yard. I didn't know where I was.

I tried to see the fallen-down parts of the house. I tried to see the stone wall that ran around the yard. I tried to see the trees on the bank of the river.

But all I could see was a wide field of tall weeds, giant plants, and huge bushes all around me.

"Lionel!" I yelled. "Lionel, where are you?"

I thought that maybe if I could hear Lionel's voice, I could figure out where the wall was. But all I could hear was the wind, whistling through the weeds in the field.

My uncle Julius had told me about being lost in the jungle. He said that he had followed a river to find his way out.

I didn't know how to find the river.
I wasn't even sure it was there at all.

I was panicking again. I looked
up and saw the bright sun. I tried to
remember where the sun had been in the
sky when I first climbed over the wall.

I was sure it had been behind me.
Maybe I would be able to find Lionel if
I walked toward the sun.

My clothes had been torn on the thorns of some of the bushes. I could feel the wind coming through the holes.

I started walking anyway. I tried not to think about the bugs buzzing all around me and hiding under all of the leaves.

I walked for a long time. For some reason, I kept feeling like I was being watched, or followed, or hunted.

When the ground was flat, I tried to speed up. I couldn't stop feeling scared. I just kept on walking.

I didn't understand why I was so scared. It didn't make any sense.

I knew people who were scared of monsters or ghosts. I was sometimes scared of dying or being hurt.

Those fears made sense. It didn't make sense to me to be afraid of a big yard. How could I explain it to Lionel once I made it out? I was so lost and so scared.

I stopped walking. "Lionel!" I yelled as loud as I could. "Lionel!"

Then I saw it. The insects weren't the only things watching me. As I watched, a hunter jumped out of the bushes.

The hunter aimed a bow at me. The arrow zoomed toward me. It flew past me, an inch from my ear!

I started to run again.

I felt like a deer must feel when hunting season comes in the fall. But at least my fear was making me run really fast!

Chapter 4

AGAINST THE WALL

I ran toward the sun. The hunter shot another arrow. That one tore my sweatshirt.

I turned back to look at the hunter. That's when I realized he wasn't just any old hunter! In fact, the hunter looked like he'd come straight from the Amazon jungle.

The hunter was just a little bit taller than me. His skin was brown.

He was not running after me. Instead, he was just walking quickly behind me, following closely.

The thorns on the bushes didn't seem to be bothering him. Neither did the tall grass or the bugs. He was walking easily through the yard.

I tried to get away from him. I ran as fast as I possibly could. But it was impossible! I knew if he shot another arrow at me, he'd get me.

I thought maybe if Lionel could hear me, or if I could hear him, I'd stop being so scared.

"Lionel!" I yelled. "Lionel!" I yelled his name at least a hundred more times, but I didn't hear anything.

My mind was running as fast as I was through the creepy yard.

Why was the hunter chasing me? Could he be trying to get the Kaan that my uncle had stolen from his people? I couldn't think of any other reason he would want to get me. But I'd lost the blue stone.

How could I give it back? How could I stop the spell that was making him hunt me?

Then I thought of something even worse. Even if I made it to the wall, if the wall still existed, how could I climb over it? While I tried to climb up the wall, the hunter would have enough time to shoot me ten times with his arrows. And if the yard had changed so much since I first saw it, what could have happened to the wall?

If it had changed as much as the yard had, the wall must be at least three hundred feet high. I was not a good climber. I was just Sam, a normal kid, who came into the yard to find his friend's ball. That's it. I wasn't a mountain climber!

I was not a long distance runner either. I could feel my heart ready to explode. I was about to stop trying.

Just then, I saw the wall, about a hundred feet away. It looked just like it had when I first climbed over it, except that Lionel was standing at the bottom. I ran over to him.

"What are you doing?" Lionel asked. He looked around. Then he added, "You know, this yard is not as small as you said it was."

Lionel looked at me and frowned. "You didn't find my ball, did you," he said. "Sam, don't tell me you lost it."

I started to cry. "I lost the stone Uncle Julius gave me," I said. "It's horrible!"

Lionel shook his head. "No, what's horrible is that you lost my ball," he told me. His voice sounded mad. "Do you know how much those balls cost?" he added, shaking his head. "And I've been waiting on the other side of the wall forever."

He didn't understand how awful the situation was. I tried to explain.

"Lionel, we'll never play ball — or anything else — ever again if we don't find that blue stone that Uncle Julius gave me," I said.

Lionel looked past me. "Who's that?" he asked. "Does he live here or something?"

I turned to look. The hunter was walking out of the bushes. He stopped and stared at us with his dark eyes. He pulled out an arrow and placed it on his bow.

I knew that Lionel and I wouldn't have time to climb over the wall. But the hunter had plenty of time to hit both of us with his arrows.

"We have to find the Kaan!" I whispered.

Lionel stared at the arrow aimed at him. Then he slowly opened his hand.

"Is this the Kaan?" he whispered. "It was right here, at the bottom of the wall. You must have dropped it when you landed here."

He held the Kaan out to me. Then he added, "Sam, who is this guy?"

I grabbed the blue stone from Lionel's hand at the same time that the hunter aimed his arrow right at me.

I threw the Kaan as hard as I could toward him. The stone and its cord spun and spun.

The arrow flew toward me. I knew I didn't have time to move.

My heart felt tight in my chest. I almost felt as though I'd already been hit by the arrow.

I had never been so scared in my whole life.

Then, as I watched, the Kaan stopped spinning. It moved toward the arrow and caught it.

The string that was holding the stone wrapped itself around the tip of the arrow, trying to slow it down, to stop it from reaching me.

I watched while the stone and the arrow fought. They were both flying toward me. If something didn't happen soon, the arrow would hit me.

Then, just before the arrow was about to strike me, the Kaan brought it down to the ground.

The Kaan had won the fight.

They lay on the ground. The Kaan's cord was still wrapped around the arrow. They were only about a foot away from my shoes.

"What was that?" Lionel whispered. "Why did that happen?"

I didn't answer him. I just leaned down and carefully unwrapped the string from the arrow.

Then I walked a few steps forward. I threw the necklace toward the hunter.

He caught it in midair and tied it around his neck. He seemed happy. Then he turned and disappeared behind the bushes and the trees.

Within a few moments, the grass, the bushes, and the trees became smaller. Some of them disappeared.

The yard was soon exactly the same as how it had looked before I climbed over the wall.

The river was on my left, flowing behind some bushes, which seemed shorter now. Just a few feet away was the broken-down old house.

And next to the house, hidden under a blackberry bush, was Lionel's ball.

Lionel walked over and grabbed his ball. "You have some explaining to do!" he said.

"There's nothing to explain," I told him. "Well, not to you, anyway. Just to Uncle Julius. He told me that the Kaan was supposed to protect hunters, but he said it was just a legend. It's not just a story! It's true! The Kaan belongs to the Amazon hunters. It's not ours!" I paused, looking around. "I knew that stone wasn't for me," I said quietly.

Then I pointed at the wall. "You go first," I said.

Before I climbed the wall, I looked back at the yard. I had never wanted to be in it to begin with. I never wanted to see it again.

I looked around for the hunter. I didn't see anyone.

That made me feel better. I knew he'd gone back to the jungle, where he and his precious stone belonged.

THE END

ABOUT THE AUTHOR

Hubert Ben Kemoun was born in 1958 in Algeria, on the northern coast of Africa. He has written plays for radio, screenplays for television, musicals for the stage, and children's books. He now lives in Nantes, France, with his wife and their two sons, Nicolas and Nathan. He likes writing detective stories, and also creates crossword puzzles for newspapers. When he writes stories, he writes them first with a pen and then copies the words onto a computer. His favorite color is black, the color of ink.

ABOUT THE ILLUSTRATOR

Thomas Ehretsmann was born in 1974 on the eastern border of France in the town of Mulhouse (pronounced mee-yoo-looz). He created his own comic strips at the age of 6, inspired by the newspapers his father read. Ehretsmann studied decorative arts in the ancient cathedral town of Strassbourg, and worked with a world-famous publisher of graphic novels, Delcourt Editions. Ehretsmann now works primarily as an illustrator of books for adults and children.

GLOSSARY

bow (BOH)—a curved piece of wood with a stretched string attached to it, used for shooting arrows

expeditions (ek-spuh-DISH-uhnz)—long trips

jungle (JUHNG-uhl)—land that is thickly covered with trees, vines, and bushes

legend (LEJ-uhnd)—a story

magical (MAJ-ik-uhl)—amazing or wonderful

miniature (MIN-ee-uh-chur)—very small

panic (PAN-ik)—a feeling of terror

patience (PAY-shuhnss)—if you have patience, you can put up with problems or delays without getting upset or angry

precious (PRESH-uhss)—rare and very special

souvenir (soo-vuh-NEER)—an object that you keep to remind you of a person, place, or event

species (SPEE-seez)—a group of animals or plants that have the same characteristics

tarantula (tuh-RAN-chuh-luh)—a large, hairy spider

thorn (THORN)—a sharp point on the branch or stem of a plant such as a rose

More About . . .

Imagine seeing a spider big enough to eat a bird. Or a snake that is longer than the width of a tennis court. The Amazon Rainforest is home to these extreme animals and much more.

The rainforest, also known as the Amazon jungle, is huge — the largest forest in the world. It lies in nine South American countries.

The Amazon faces a major threat today. Much of the forest is being lost to deforestation.

In this process, forests are cleared and trees are cut down. Often the cleared land is farmed or developed into communities.

THE AMAZON RAINFOREST

If deforestation continues at the current rate, then 40 percent of the rainforest will be gone within 20 years. As the forest disappears, so will many of the plants and animals.

In addition to massive tarantulas and snakes, many other species of animals are found in the Amazon. They include:

- 2.5 million insect species
- 3,000 fish species
- nearly 1,300 bird species
- more than 420 mammal species
- nearly 440 amphibian species
- about 380 reptile species

Discussion Questions

1. Why do you think Uncle Julius gave the Kaan to Sam? Why did Sam have to give it back? Was it wrong of Uncle Julius to take it? Talk about your answers.

2. Why did the backyard appear to get bigger? What were some of the other changes that happened? Why did the changes take place?

3. As a group, talk about the Amazon rain forest. What do you know about it? What other books have you read about it? Do you know any movies about it? Talk about what you know.

WRITING PROMPTS

1. What would have happened if Lionel hadn't found the Kaan? Write a new ending to this book.

2. Uncle Julius goes on lots of amazing adventures. Choose a place in the world where you have never been. Then, pretending to be Uncle Julius, write a postcard to your nephew, Sam, telling him all about your trip.

3. Imagine that Uncle Julius had brought Sam a different present. What do you think he could have brought Sam? Write a story in which Uncle Julius gives Sam something else.

INTERNET SITES

Do you want to know more about subjects related to this book? Or are you interested in learning about other topics? Then check out FactHound, a fun, easy way to find Internet sites.

Our investigative staff has already sniffed out great sites for you!

Here's how to use FactHound:

1. Visit *www.facthound.com*

2. Select your grade level.

3. To learn more about subjects related to this book, type in the book's ISBN number: 9781434212214.

4. Click the Fetch It button.

FactHound will fetch the best Internet sites for you!